Yesterday's Crush

Susan Horsnell

USA Today Bestselling Author

Contents

No 1 Best Sellers in 2018:

Matt—Book 1 in The Carter Brothers Series

Clay—Book 3 in The Carter Brothers Series

No 1 Best Seller in February 2019

Andrew's Outback Love—Book 1 in The Outback Australia Series

No 1 Best Seller in July 2019

Ruby's Outback Love—Book 2 in The Outback Australia Series

No 1 Best Seller in May 2019

Eight Letters

Will—Book 2 in The Carter Brothers Series

Best Seller in April 2020

Cora: Bride of South Dakota

YESTERDAY'S CRUSH

Copyright © 2021 by Susan Horsnell

This story is set in Australia and written in Australian English.

Edited: Redline Editing

Proofread: Leanne Rogers

Published by: Lipstick Publishing

ABN: 573-575-99847

Cover by Kellie Cover Designs

https://www.facebook.com/kellie.theresa.56

Chapter One

December 12th

The wind blew hard, the sky darkening and threatening a typical summer storm, but Lyndsay left the marked track that headed to the waterfall and quietly followed the baby kangaroo along the edge of the mountain. The baby was moving with an unsteady gait; it appeared to be injured.

I'll only follow for a few minutes and then I'll hurry back to the car, she told herself.

The clouds burst without warning; and torrential rain had her drenched within seconds. Lyndsay shivered as she pushed into the wind, trying desperately to return to the marked track.

Fear raced through her body as the ground beneath her feet rumbled.

Landslide!

She started to run, adrenaline pushing her back the way she'd come. It was too little too late. The ground beneath her slid away, and she tumbled head over heels as she was carried away by what had once been a mountainside. Acres of mud and rubble accelerated her fall, pushing her along. Litres of water washed over her, generated by the pouring rain. She spluttered and coughed, trying desperately to breathe. The backpack pounded into her back as she rolled. Lyndsay knew she was in a shitload of trouble.

Her fall was brought to a temporary stop when a branch, still attached to a tree stump, seemed to reach out and grab her by the ankle, twisting it painfully. It had prevented her from tumbling further, but moments later she heard a loud snap, and was sent hurtling toward the river below.

Lyndsay hit the water, the force almost knocking the air from her lungs, and sank below the surface. The backpack dragged her down and she fought to rid herself of the weight. Once freed, her head bobbed above the water. She was being dragged rapidly down river and knew she needed to find a way out of the raging water before she was knocked unconscious by debris rushing in all directions

Doing what she'd been taught to do by her father, Lyndsay swam with the rapidly flowing water and inched her way closer to the bank on the opposite side. An overhanging tree came within reach and she threw herself onto one of the branches. Water swirled around her ankles and pain shot up the leg of the ankle she'd injured causing her to cry out and almost release the tenuous hold she had on the tree.

Forget about the pain, you have to get out of the water to safety.

Lyndsay inched her way through the branches of the tree until she was within reach of the steep bank. Unpeeling her fingers from the wooden savior, she sucked in a deep breath and threw herself onto the firm ground. Pain shot through her leg, but she needed to get to higher ground before the tide rose and she found herself back in the river.

Lyndsay crawled upwards, dragging her leg with what she suspected was a broken ankle behind her. Tears mixed with the rainwater which relentlessly pelted down.

Why did I stray from the track?

She asked herself the question for about the hundredth time, but deep down she knew why. When an animal appeared to be in distress, there was no choice for her but to do what she could to help.

At that moment, she was bearing the consequences of her miscalculated actions. An experienced hiker, Lyndsay knew anything could happen when you were out in the bush, she should have remained on the well-established track.

How many times had she drummed into her Boy Scout team; that they must stay on the marked paths?

Like always, without thinking, she'd been prepared to take the risk to rescue the little kangaroo. An animal lover all her life, what else could she have done?

Scanning the area, relief spread through her body when a cave opening with a large entry ledge about two metres from the top of the ravine caught her eye.

Lindsay crawled toward the ledge and hefted herself inside the cave. Finally out of the rain, and being exhausted after crawling around six metres uphill, she flopped onto her back and closed her eyes. The steep uphill crawl had sapped every ounce of her energy. She was wet, freezing, and covered in mud.

On the opposite side of the river from the marked track which led to Samson Bay and the waterfall, Lyndsay knew she was in deep trouble. With what she thought was a badly broken ankle, there was no way of getting herself out of the ravine to safety.

What if no-one can find me?

It was less than two weeks until Christmas, and there was still so much to be done. Thoughts drifted to her three-year-old son, Dylan, and the fun they'd had together while putting up the tree. She'd lifted him into her arms, and he'd been so careful, as he'd placed the fragile angel on top. They'd giggled as parcels were shaken, and guesses made about the contents, before placing them beneath the tree. Would she never see him again? He was her last thought before she passed out.

***

Rick pushed the button at the pedestrian crossing lights, and while he waited for them to change for red to green, a poster tacked to a pole caught his eye.

He stepped closer to the pole while squinting to take a closer look at the picture at the top of the poster. The unsettled stormy weather of the past couple of days had taken its toll, and the paper was tattered, but he could still make out the familiar, pretty face gazing back at him. He fought the wind to straighten the paper so he could read what was written.

Missing since December 12. Lyndsay Richards. Aged 22.

Lyndsay Richards. That was a name he hadn't heard since they'd been students at Narrabeen High, four years earlier.

The image on the poster brought back memories, and feelings, of a crush he'd thought long buried.

Rick had been besotted with the gorgeous blonde haired, blue eyed girl who had represented the school in Netball. He'd spent many hours sitting in the stands admiring her as she ran from one end of the court to the other. The skirt she wore dancing over her rear end, and showing off her long, slender legs. But it wasn't only her looks that had caused him to be smitten, she had been a genuinely nice girl.

It had been painful leaving his crush behind when they'd left school. He, to head into the Police Force. Lindsay? Rick had no idea.

Gorgeous women like Lyndsay Richards didn't give people like him the time of day. She hadn't known he'd existed because Rick had made sure he wasn't noticed.

While she had been tall, slim, beautiful, and athletic, he had been short, chubby, and a nerd.

An old lady patted his hand. "Sir, the light's green. We can cross now."

He was startled from his thoughts and dropped his head to gaze into the eyes of a small, feeble-looking old lady. "Sorry, ma'am. Would you like me to assist you to cross the road?"

"No thank you, Officer, I'm quite capable of managing the crossing myself. I just didn't know if you realized the light had changed. You seemed to be a million miles away." She smiled before setting off to cross the road.

Rick hesitated before turning his attention back to the poster. Lyndsay had been missing since December 12, it was now December 15.

The damage to the poster, caused by the inclement weather, meant a description of Lyndsay was barely readable and half of the Crimestoppers contact number was missing.

Three days. She could be anywhere. I'll check on the computer back at the station and see if there's been any news of her whereabouts.

He spun on his heels and headed back to the Police Station in Halmat. Lunch could wait.

Rick addressed his partner who was seated at his desk studying something on the computer in front of him. "Gavin, do you know anything about a young woman missing in the Narrabeen area? Any reports come in from them, or requests to help with the search?"

He munched on a salad sandwich, but hearing Rick's question, he tilted his head and looked up.

"That pretty blonde on the posters that are stuck up everywhere around town? As far as I know, she's still missing and there's been nothing from the guys up at Narrabeen. What's your interest?"

"I used to go to school with her. A poster drew my attention as I was about to cross Central Avenue. Do you know who's looking after her case?"

"No idea. Since the national park is closest to the Narrabeen station, it would have to be a couple of detectives from there."

"I might give them a call. See what information they can give me. It's been three days, maybe they found her."

"We're quiet at the moment, and you're due to knock off anyway, why don't you go over and see them? We have the next couple of days off, you could offer to help out?"

"Yeah, I will. Thanks mate."

"Rick."

"Yeah."

"Who exactly is she? Were you a couple at school?"

Rick laughed. "Me? No way. Lyndsay was tall and absolutely gorgeous. Blue eyes, hair like gold silk. She wouldn't have given me a second glance. To be fair, she seemed to be very sweet, but I never had the courage to approach her."

Gavin was puzzled. Rick was the epitome of a tall, dark, and handsome guy that every girl dreamed about. He worked out every morning and night, and had the muscular torso to prove it.

Rick laughed again at the puzzled expression on his partner's face. "In high school, I was short, overweight, pimply, and the text book example of a nerd."

Gavin raised his eyebrows at his partner and best friends' confession. "I didn't know."

"No, it's not something I brag about. I worked hard to get a decent body, nature took care of the rest."

"Go find her, mate."

Rick patted Gavin on the shoulder. "I'll certainly try. I only hope she's alive. Have a good couple of days with Sandy and the kids. Say hi for me and tell her I'll see them Christmas Day."

"I will. I can't wait to tell her you were an ugly duckling that turned into a swan."

Rick chuckled before heading for the lift that would take him to his car in the underground carpark.

As he unlocked his bright red Mazda MX-5, something gnawed at his gut. Something wasn't right. What had happened to Lindsay, and where was she?

***

Rick waved to the Sergeant at the front desk as he strode past toward the Detective's part of the station. It wasn't unusual for police in uniform to be given access to other stations.

Rick knew where he was going, he'd been there before. He passed through a glass door into the large area used by the detectives and glanced around.

A man and woman were huddled together and hunched over a computer screen; no-one else was around. He cleared his throat as he approached. The pair finally looked up.

"Can we help you?" the female asked as she raked her eyes over the Senior Constable before her.

Rick twirled his police cap in his hands. "I'm Senior Constable Rick Masters from Halmat." He presented his hand and the female shook first.

"Senior Detective Janine Kelly."

"Senior Detective Mark Greene. Have a seat and tell us what can we do for you?"

Chairs scraped across the tiled floor as they pulled three into a circle and sat down.

"I noticed a poster of a young woman on a crossing pole down in Halmat. She's been missing for the past three days and I wondered who was handling the investigation." Rick's eyes moved back and forth between the two.

"Lyndsay Richards, she's been missing for three days," Mark stated.

"Yes."

"What's your interest?" Janine sounded a little defensive.

"We were at school together and I was curious to know if she'd been found."

"Not yet. She disappeared while bushwalking in the Kalamba National Park. Apparently, her and the boyfriend had an argument and broke up. She was upset and her parents said she mentioned going hiking for the day. When she hadn't returned by late afternoon, her parents became worried and went to search for her. They found her car in the parking area at the entrance to the Samson Bay Waterfall track but no sign of their daughter anywhere. Her father told us, it was out of character for her to be missing, and apparently when she's feeling down, the waterfall track is her favourite to hike."

"I assume you've searched the track?" Rick asked.

"Yes, we have, but bad weather and a landslide have prevented us from searching the entire track and some of the surrounding area. It's too unstable and dangerous. We brought in a highly experienced bush search and rescue team, but they turned up nothing, and now they're needed elsewhere due to damage caused by storms. We're down to one search crew of about fifteen from National Parks and Wildlife, and they're checking out some of the safer trails that leave from the same carpark until we can get the other team back. We also have about thirty police combing where it's safe, but there are dozens of aboriginal caves that we know about in the area, and to be honest, it will take weeks to search them all. Due to the landslide, we can't access some and there may be caves we don't know exist."

Rick was familiar with the area, and knew what Janine said was true.

"I have the next two days off, and I know the area well. Do you mind if I take a look?"

Mark nodded. "No, we'd appreciate any help we can get. With the bad storms of the past few days, we haven't been able to utilize Search and Rescue as much as we would like because of all the damage to homes in the area. They are doing their best with limited manpower. National Parks and Wildlife are short staffed, but they have been doing all they can. They were the ones who told us there could be dozens of caves that haven't yet been found and documented."

"What about the local Aboriginals?" Rick asked.

"The Garrigal people. We have spoken to some of their descendants, but none of them are familiar with the complete cave system and weren't able to help. The entire park has suffered so much storm damage that the teams are restricted in where they can search safely. We can't risk sending them into the zone where the landslide occurred, it's too dangerous. We need highly experienced and skilled people, and until we get our bush team back, we have to avoid the area." Frustration sounded in Mark's voice.

"Why the hell are they using a highly experienced bush crew to clean up storm damage in suburbia?"

Mark shrugged. Just following orders from higher up the chain."

"Do you have a contact for someone I can speak with?"

"Adam Bertana." Janine wrote the contact number on a sheet of paper and handed it to Rick. He folded it and placed it in the top pocket of his uniform shirt.

"Would it be okay if I talked with Lyndsay's parents?" Rick spoke tentatively, not wanting to step on the Detective's toes.

"Can't see why not," Mark wrote their numbers on another sheet of paper.

Rick folded it and placed it with the other one. "Anything else you can tell me?" he asked as he stood.

"That's about all we know. We've checked with the boyfriend, and her other friends, but no-one seems to know anything and no one has heard from her. Calls to

Lyndsay's mobile phone haven't been answered but she probably wouldn't have had any reception and the battery would be flat by now. We had tracker dogs in the area, but they were hampered by rain and fallen debris, so they came up empty as well. We're stumped. It's like she's vanished into thin air." Mark stood and offered his hand. "I've written mine and Janine's number on the sheet with Lyndsay's parents' numbers. Call us if you find anything."

"Will do." Rick again shook their hands, thanked them, and left.

Chapter Two

Tears streamed down Lyndsay's face. She was cold, wet, hungry, and in pain. Her ankle felt like a dozen knives were being plunged into the bone.

The sun was again dipping beyond the horizon. She'd lost track of how many days and nights she had spent in the cave due to being in and out of consciousness. Thank heavens she had managed to crawl to the cave. Without the protection it gave, she would have been exposed to the fierce storms and more than likely would not have survived as long.

The couple of muesli bars she'd shoved in her pockets before setting out were almost gone, but she'd managed to gather rainwater on large leaves to keep herself from dying of thirst. She had managed to keep herself alive, but was she only delaying the inevitable?

A fresh batch of tears cascaded over her cheeks. Her ankle screamed in pain, the joint swollen and lying at a strange angle. Gut instinct warned her that if she attempted to walk, she would be in danger of causing irreparable damage and maybe losing her foot. With this in mind, she'd been holed up in the cave with her leg elevated on a rock. When she had needed to relieve herself, she crawled out of the cave to one side of the ledge and then back again.

Surely her parents would have reported her missing and a search would have been instigated? If they were searching, how would they find her? She was so far from the original track which was now on the other side of a ravine.

Think, Lyndsay, think. You need to do something to help yourself.

***

Rick glanced around as he knocked on the door of the Victorian era brick home in Narrabeen. The gardens were full of colorful plants and the lawns immaculately tended.

A middle-aged man threw the door open, and the minute he set eyes on Rick dressed in his police uniform, he paled.

"Mr Richards, please don't be alarmed. I just wanted to ask you a couple of questions. I'm Senior Constable Rick Masters. I know your daughter from school. Or rather, I did.. It's been a long time."

Alex Richards exhaled with visible relief and the two men shook hands. "Come on in and please call me Alex."

Rick followed him along a hall and into the living room where he was offered a seat. He folded his body into a soft, velvet covered chair, and placed his police cap on his knee.

"Can I get you anything?" Alex asked.

"I'm fine thanks," Rick answered.

"I'll get my wife, Joan. Won't be a minute."

Rick observed his surroundings while he sat waiting. The living room was beautifully decorated in shades of off-white and beige. Sumptuous chairs matched a three-seater lounge; the coffee table and display cabinet were constructed from solid white oak. Money oozed from his surroundings. He had always suspected Lyndsay's family were wealthy, not that it mattered.

A little boy rushed into the room and plonked his arms across Rick's knees. "A real live policeman!"

Rick laughed and set his hat on the little boy's mop of blond hair.

"That little bundle of energy is our grandson—Dylan. We've been taking care of him for the past few days." Alex smiled at the child fondly as he spoke, but Rick didn't miss the cloud of worry that crossed the older man's face.

A woman, an older version of the Lyndsay he'd seen on the poster, entered the room. Rick stood and addressed her.

"Mrs Richards, I'm Senior Constable Rick Masters from the Halmat Station."

Joan darted a look of concern at her husband.

"The Senior Constable is a friend of Lyndsay's from school. He wants to ask us a few questions."

"Please, call me, Joan. Rick Masters, you said? I don't recall Lyndsay having a friend by that name when she was at school." She took a seat by her husband and admired the hat Dylan insisted on showing her.

Rick sat back down. "I wasn't a friend, and I haven't seen her since school, but I did know her."

"Pity, she could have done well knowing you instead of that ratbag, no hoper she was with. Got her pregnant before he disappeared leaving her with nothing but a bunch of debts to be paid. Even cleaned out her bank account. Oh well, I guess we wouldn't have this little fellow if she hadn't met him, so it's not all bad." Joan ruffled Dylan's blond hair.

Dylan is Lyndsay's son. I should have known with that blond hair and her blue eyes. I have to find her, he can't lose his mother.

Rick had lost his mother in an accident when he was only four years old so the thought of the little boy losing his cut to the bone. His stepmother had been wonderful, but it wasn't the same.

"What can we help you with Officer?" Alex asked.

"Call me Rick, please. I have a couple of days off and I know the park better than most people. I spend a lot of time hiking the tracks."

"It's surprising you haven't seen Lyndsay on one of them." I agreed with Alex, it was intriguing that we hadn't run across each other, but the national park covered thousands of hectares so it was understandable.

"It's a huge area, I should imagine there are a number of hikers I've never crossed paths with. Or should I say tracks? Anyway, I thought if you didn't object, I'd head up there and search for your daughter. It would be as a civilian member of the public not in my official capacity as a Police Officer."

"Of course we don't object," Joan said eagerly. "The more people out there searching for her, the better chance we have of getting our daughter back, and if you know the area, you'll know best where to look."

Rick nodded. "I was told her car was parked in the carpark on West Head Road. Do you know if she was definitely going along the Samson Bay Track? There are a couple of tracks from there and I want to check the most likely one first."

"She was terribly upset when she dropped Dylan off to us. Her latest boyfriend had broken up with her. No loss if you ask us, but she was hurt nonetheless. He insisted he didn't want her *and* Dylan. She said she needed some quiet time to herself to think and reassess the direction her life was headed. She told us she was going to hike down to the waterfall for a swim and would be back by late afternoon." Her Dad's voice shook as he spoke. "Lindsay's an expert hiker, Rick, something must be terribly wrong because she would have never gotten lost. Please find her."

"I'll do my best. Fortunately I've hiked that area myself on many occasions and know it well. Rick stood. "Thank you for your time and confirming where she could be before I head out. I promise I'll find her for you, and for Dylan."

With the little fella involved, Rick knew this 'case' had just become a whole lot more personal.

Dylan crooked his finger at Rick, who crouched down. The little boy gazed into his face. "Mr Officer, are you a secret Santa? Mummy said Santa is a secret man who lives at the North Pole. He has lots of elves around the world who tell him when boys and girls have been good. And he has secret Santas all around the world that help him sometimes because he can't be everywhere at once. Mummy said once a year, Santa brings special things to boys and girls who have been really good. I've been really, really good and my Mummy's special. Are you going to bring her home for Christmas?"

Rick's heart thundered in his chest and he gathered the little boy into a hug. Tears burned his eyes. "I'll be your very own secret Santa and find your Mummy. I promise she'll be home for Christmas." He hoped it was a promise he could keep.

Dylan set the hat back on Rick's head before running to his Grandma. "Ganma, the policeman is secret Santa. He's going to find Mummy so you don't have to be sad."

Joan scooped him up onto her lap. Tears pricked her eyes. "Yes darling, the nice policeman will try his best to find Mummy and bring her home."

Joan gazed up at Rick, pleading for the safe return of Lyndsay was evident in her tear soaked eyes.

Alex showed Rick to the door where he said goodbye and descended the steps to his car. He slipped behind the wheel and fired up the engine.

Please God, help me find her and bring her home for Christmas.

***

Rick drove his vehicle into the car park of the unit block, switched off the motor, slid from the seat, and locked up. He crossed to the lift, stepped inside, and pushed the button for the fifth floor as the doors closed. A bell dinged when it arrived at the destination. He stepped from the car into the carpeted hallway, turned left to his apartment and unlocked the door.

His unit was cozy; two bedrooms, spacious living room, and a kitchen. Although not large, he loved both it and the location.

He could sit on his balcony and both watch, and listen to, the waves as they crashed onto the shore below. The unit had been a legacy from his Grandmother and he could still feel her spirit within. He often spoke to her out loud when he was troubled and he felt she had guided his decisions on more than one occasion. He needed her now more than ever.

After throwing his keys in a bowl on the kitchen table, Rick strode to his bedroom where he changed into sweats and a T-shirt.

After grabbing his laptop from the kitchen table, and a can of cola from the fridge, he unlocked the glass door which led onto the balcony. He stood for a moment, breathing in the crisp salt air and watching surfers battle the waves.

Rick had never learned to surf, his father always worked long hours and had been too busy to teach him. Rick hadn't minded, he'd been more interested in reading books about the law and was now in his fourth year of studying to become a lawyer. One day he wanted his own legal practice.

He placed his drink on the balcony table and dialed a number from the sheet he'd been given by Mark and Janine.

"Adam Bertana." The deep voice rumbled down the line.

"Mr Bertana, my name is Rick Masters. I'm a friend of Lyndsay Richards."

"The girl who's missing in Kalamba. Detectives in Narrabeen told us about her and asked about the caves in the national park."

"I have the next couple of days off from Halmat station and was wondering if you could give me a hand to search where the landslide occurred?" Rick crossed his fingers. He knew the park well, like the back of his hand actually, but still not as well as the local aborigines.

There was silence from the other end of the phone. "Mr. Bertana?"

"If we're going to spend the next couple of days together you better call me, Adam."

"You'll help?"

"Of course. Sorry for the delay in answering, I was checking my diary. I don't have anything urgent on until the weekend, so I'll have my meetings rescheduled. I'd be happy to help you. Where do you want to meet me and what time?"

"In the car park at the entrance to the Samson Bay Track. 6 am too early?"

"Perfect. I'll see you tomorrow."

"Thanks, Adam." Rick disconnected the phone. He was feeling much more positive now he knew he'd have experienced help.

He flashed up his laptop and Googled information and studied images of damage done by the landslide to walking tracks in the park. For the rest of the night, he examined topographic maps of the terrain to refresh his knowledge. He would be well prepared by the time he met Adam the following day.

***

"You are obviously Adam," Rick stepped from his car and offered his hand to the tall man.

"Yep, that's me. Since we're the only two here now the search and rescue team have headed off, you must be Rick."

"Got it in one." Rick pulled on his backpack filled with food, water, several ropes, and a first aid kit. Adam also picked his pack up from the ground near where he stood and settled it onto his back. Rick suspected he was just as well equipped.

The day had dawned bright, and warmth from the still rising sun was already clearing the mist of the morning, as they stepped onto the bush track.

They were surrounded by scribbly gum trees, wattle, acacias, and a myriad of other plants as they slowly trudged north.

Adam kept his eyes fixed on the ground and surrounding bush. "I doubt there will be any tracks after the storms, but it doesn't hurt to look."

"Do you know the park well?" Rick asked.

"Better than most people, but not as well as my ancestors. Sometimes I bring groups of kids through and show them the ancient carvings in caves that were done by my people hundreds, maybe thousands of years ago."

"I've seen engravings of the woman with the whale and shark, also one of a goanna. You get a sense of the presence of the ancient people when you take the time to rest there."

Adam glanced up at Rick. "Yes. As an aboriginal I feel it, but it's unusual for a white man to also feel their presence. It shows respect for my people that you can."

They continued downhill in silence, scouring the landscape and calling Lyndsay's name. Apart from lizards and other small critters scurrying about, they heard and found nothing.

Parks and Wildlife, along with police, were on the other side of the ridge line as Mark had advised they would be the previous day. They repeatedly called out Lyndsay's name and the sound floated to Rick and Adam on the light breeze.

The area the two men now picked their way over had been partially searched by highly trained professionals who'd found nothing, but Rick felt in his gut that Lyndsay was nearby.

They approached a section of the track that weaved its way down the mountainside to the base of the waterfall, but carnage off to their left, about five metres away from where they stood, snagged their interest. They approached cautiously to where a once narrow ravine, around six metres deep, had been transformed into a yawning slash in the landscape. The river rushing below pushed along a tangled mess of debris. They stopped and took a long look around.

"Landslide was a big one," Adam noted.

"It's even worse than the satellite images showed." Rick's heart thumped against his ribs and his stomach back flipped.

He had so many questions…

What if Lyndsay had left the path leading to the waterfall and been caught in the slide?

Had she gone over the cliff edge?

Was she dead, or was she lying injured somewhere?

…and no answers.

Chapter Three

The early morning sun warmed Lyndsay's cold, weary body as she sat on the ledge outside the cave, scanning her surroundings, and pondering the future. Or lack thereof.

The area had been decimated by fierce storms. It was obvious from the destruction around her, that the landslide which had caused her accident, hadn't been the only one. The entire landscape had been rearranged. Fallen trees and debris lay in random piles for as far as the eyes could see. Huge sections of the mountain had collapsed into the raging river below.

Lyndsay's stomach grumbled in protest, she had eaten the last morsels of food earlier in the morning. With her ankle now slightly blue, and three times its normal size, she couldn't even scavenge for bush food.

I'm gonna die. All they'll find will be a pile of bones.

Lyndsay dropped her head into her hands and cried. She didn't want to die in the wilderness alone. Dylan needed her.

Sure, her parents would take good care of her son, but it wasn't the same. She tilted her head back and gazed up at the clear blue sky. "Why isn't somebody coming?" She screamed in frustration. "I can't do this any longer, I need help."

She lay down on the ledge, too weak to fight anymore and believing her situation was hopeless.

"Goodbye my sweet, innocent Dylan. Goodbye Mum and Dad. I love you all so much."

As wildlife scurried around her, Lyndsay allowed darkness to sweep her away. Perhaps for the last time.

***

Rick and Adam sat on rocks near the edge of a ravine where a wide stretch of bushland had once been. They perused the changed landscape as they devoured sandwiches and guzzled water. The sun was high in the sky and the conditions were steamy and hot. It was typical summer weather.

"Where do you suggest we try next? Should we continue down to the falls?" Rick asked Adam.

Adam sat quietly thinking for a moment. "My gut is telling me she didn't go down the track. She left it for some reason, but I'm still not convinced the slide swept her into the river. She wouldn't have survived and I sense her presence somewhere close. I think we should walk the edge of the ravine, check any ledges below."

"Beginning here?" Rick pointed in front of the rock where he was seated.

"Yeah. There are a lot of trees in the path of the slide that are still in place. They've suffered damage but have remained entrenched in the earth along the edges of the ravine. *If* she was caught up when the ground broke away, she might have been lucky enough to grab hold of one. She could be hidden beneath a ledge or might have crawled into a cave. Keep your eyes peeled for either. If you spot a cave, we'll find a way to check it out."

Rick voiced his fear. "But if she hasn't gone over in the slide, why hasn't she turned up? Her parents indicated she's an experienced hiker, and although it looks bad, she would have been able to drag herself out."

"Maybe she was caught on the edge of the slide and was injured by falling debris. If she was hit by something, she could be holed up waiting for help." Adam wasn't doing a very good job of reassuring his companion.

"Maybe." Rick wasn't convinced.

They packed all their rubbish into their backpacks, and as afternoon closed in, they began a methodical search, peering down along the jagged edges of the newly formed ravine.

They covered the ground, for hours, searching centimetre by centimetre until the temperature began dropping and the light dimmed. They'd found nothing.

"Time we called it a day," Adam told Rick.

"Let's check up ahead first." Rick wasn't ready to call it a day.

"Alright, but we need to make it quick. We're a fair distance from the track and I don't want to try and negotiate the way back in the dark."

The two men traipsed through the dense bush in silence. Moments later, Adam glimpsed something red in the dull, fading light.

"What's that?" He pointed to the other side of the gaping opening in the earth to where a splash of bright red, about ten metres off to their right, was illuminated by the last of the sun's rays.

"What's what?"

Adam rushed ahead to higher ground. "Look, over there. Something red. Looks like clothing. Could be her."

The men dashed through the bush which scratched and tore at Rick's legs. He didn't care. If there was a chance it was Lyndsay lying out there, he had to get to her.

They stood on the edge of where the ground had fallen away, opposite where they'd first sighted the splash of red. The collapse had widened the once narrow ravine, and it was now more than four metres across.

Despite the fact small bushes and trees obscured their view, Rick could see it was a female's body on the other side. He instinctively knew it was Lyndsay.

"Lyndsay!" Rick shouted.

There was no response, she remained motionless

"Lyndsay!" He shouted again.

Nothing.

"We have to find a way to get to her, Adam."

"Do you have your mobile phone?"

Rick pulled it from his pocket and spun around. Extending his arm he held it up, down, but there was no signal this deep into the park. "No service."

"Okay. Let's think." The men walked in circles, peering into the ravine. The river below seemed to laugh up at them, mocking the fact they were stopped cold by the raging waters below. There was no way of crossing to the other side from where they stood.

Adam thought for a moment. "The only thing we can do is head up the hill, to where the old rope bridge crosses the ravine and hope it wasn't involved in the slide. If it was, we'll have to helicopter in; there's no other way to cross the river."

"Fine, let's go." Rick hurriedly followed the edge of the ravine, pushing thick bush out of his way as he proceeded.

"It's gonna be dark soon, we need to head back." Adam was becoming concerned, the bush could be deadly at night.

Rick stopped and spun to face him. "I'm not leaving Lyndsay out here alone for another night. I have a flashlight, food, and water. You head back and alert the emergency services to come get us in the morning." He pulled a paper from his pocket. "These are her parents contact details and the detective's names at the Narrabeen station. Can you let them all know?"

"Yeah, but I'm not sure about leaving, Rick. What if you fall or get injured? You don't even know it's her."

"Who else would it be? I don't know of any other women who are missing that could be out here. I'm staying. You can decide what you want to do, but we're wasting time, and I need to get to her."

"Okay. I'll head back and call it in but be careful." Adam reached into his backpack and removed a bottle of water, some muesli bars, and a sandwich which he handed to Rick. "I'll see you in the morning."

Adam headed in the direction of the track. "Be careful," Rick called to his back.

Rick worked his way through the dense bush. The light was fading fast now that the sun had almost dropped behind the horizon. The thought of Lyndsay being hurt, and alone, propelled him along. He prayed he didn't become lost in the semi-darkness.

Finally, the rope bridge across the ravine came into view, he'd never been more relieved to see it was intact. As he headed in the direction of the bridge, he stumbled over loose rocks and tripped on hidden branches; falling to his knees on more than one occasion as he picked his way along in the darkness.

Despite being summer, it had become cold caused by a chill wind blowing off the surrounding mountains. He took the time to stop and pulled his all-weather jacket from his pack, slipped it on, and zipped it up to his chin. His flashlight scanned ahead as he raced across wooden planks held by ropes which formed the rickety bridge.

There…I can see the red again. Hold on Lyndsay, I'm coming.

He hurried as fast as he could, picking his way carefully down to the ledge until he reached Lyndsay's side and dropped to his knees. He shone the light over her, checking for injuries.

She was filthy, covered in dirt and dried blood from a myriad of cuts and scratches, her lips cracked and burnt, hair a tangled mess, but he'd never seen a more beautiful sight. He shook her gently.

"Lyndsay, wake up honey."

***

Someone was shaking her and calling her name. Had she arrived in heaven?

"Open your eyes for me, honey."

The voice again—a deep, rumbling voice, filled with kindness, but she wanted to sleep. She wasn't ready for heaven.

"Lyndsay, come on. Open your eyes."

The shaking became more insistent and she swatted at his hand in anger.

"Leave me alone. I want to sleep." Her voice sounded scratchy and weak.

The man stopped shaking her when she spoke. Cracking one eye open, she watched as he reached into his backpack and pulled out a first aid kit. "Where are you hurt?"

"Everywhere," she mumbled while closing her eye.

"Can you sit up?"

"No, I want to sleep." Her stomach growled loudly.

"Lyndsay, I need you to open your eyes and look at me. I have food and water, but you can't have them until I know you're awake and can sit up."

"Why do I need food and water in heaven?"

"Honey, you're not in heaven. You're in the National Park. We have been searching for you."

Has someone found me? I'm not dead? Dylan! I'll be home for Christmas with Dylan.

Slowly she peeled her eyes open and peered into her rescuer's face. Such a kind, handsome face. "Who are you?"

"My name is Rick...Rick Masters." He ran his hands gently over her body causing all sorts of conflicting emotions.

"I can't feel any obvious injuries or broken bones. Where do you hurt?"

"Rick Masters," she murmured. *Why does that name sound familiar?*

"Why couldn't you get out of the park?"

"Couldn't walk—broken ankle." She winced as he helped her to sit up.

He shone the light down on her feet. Her right ankle was swollen and puffy, the skin stretched so tight, it looked like it was ready to pop.

"I'm no medic but I'd say your ankle is badly broken. I have help coming in the morning and they'll have a stretcher to carry you out."

"Thank you. Can I have water, please?"

He handed her a bottle of water, and she gulped thirstily before wiping the back of her hand across her mouth, catching stray droplets.

"Thank you, for finding me."

"You're very welcome, honey." He waved the flashlight around and fixed the light on the entrance to the cave behind them. "Have you been in the cave?"

"Yes, I sheltered in there out of the storm. When the weather cleared, I came back out so anyone searching would be able to see where I was. I must have passed out again."

"Your parents said you were an experienced hiker and were headed to the waterfall at Samson Bay. What are you doing on this side of the river? What happened to you?" He angled the flashlight up off the ground and wiped her face over with sterile wipes from the first aid kit.

"There was an injured baby kangaroo and I was hoping to help the little critter. Then the landslide hit. As I was being pushed toward the edge by rocks and mud, a branch from a tree snagged me by the foot. That's what broke my ankle. When the branch snapped, the mud and rocks took me over and into the river. I swam to an overhanging tree, hauled myself out of the water and crawled up here where I saw the cave."

Rick paled on hearing how close Lyndsay had come to losing her life. "Sounds like were extremely fortunate to escape with only a broken ankle and a few small cuts and bruises."

"I'm grateful to be alive." Lyndsay burst into tears and Rick held her close as she sobbed, soothing her until she quieted.

Once settled, he spread ointment over the cuts and scrapes to help stave off any infection.

When Lyndsay shivered with cold, or maybe shock, he became concerned.

"Let's get you into the cave, I have a small exposure blanket in the first aid kit which will help keep you warm."

She intended to roll over to crawl back to the cave, but Rick stood, scooped her into his arms, and carried her inside. Her head rested against his broad chest. For the first time in days, she felt safe. He carefully set her down on the cave floor.

"I'll get my pack and be straight back." He disappeared into the darkness but reappeared seconds later.

Rick dropped to his knees beside Lyndsay and pulled a foil blanket from his pack.

"Here, wrap this around you and it'll help keep you warm." He draped the blanket over her shoulders and pulled it tightly around her slim frame. He held it together just below her neck. "Hold it here while I'll get a safety pin from the first aid kit."

He lifted one of her hands to guide her to where the ends met. "Your fingers are like ice." Rick rubbed her hands briskly between his own until they felt a bit warmer before securing the ends of the blanket in place with a safety pin.

"Thank you," she murmured.

"Do you think you could eat something? I have some ham and cheese sandwiches and a couple of muesli bars."

"I would love a sandwich and some more water." Lyndsay felt dehydrated after lying under the beating sun all day.

Rick pulled out a pack with the sandwiches and handed her half. He watched her closely as they sat eating quietly.

Why is he looking like he wants to devour me?

Lyndsay lifted a bottle of water to her lips and drank thirstily before screwing the lid back into place and setting it down on the ground.

"Your name's familiar, have I met you before?"

Rick cringed, but she had no idea why.

He took a deep breath before answering. "I was kinda hoping you wouldn't remember me. We attended Narrabeen High School and took the same English and Science classes."

"I don't remember you." Her eyes dragged over his body. He was the tallest, most handsome man, she'd ever met. He had a voice that washed over her like warm water, and even in the dim light, she noticed his piercing blue eyes.

I'd never forget you if we'd met before.

"Are you sure you have the right Lyndsay?"

"Yeah. I was a pretty forgettable kid in high school, so it doesn't surprise me that you don't remember who I am."

"Rick Masters….why is your name so familiar?" Somewhere, in the back of her mind, the name rang a bell.

Rick must have seen her confusion and decided to put her out of her misery.

"Picture this. Short, hair that looked like it was cut around a bowl—because it was, glasses, pimples, overweight, well known as a clumsy nerd."

She raised a hand to her mouth. "*That* Rick Masters."

"Yep. That was me."

"Oh, you used to sit up in the back of the stands and watch me play netball. You were always alone. I don't think I ever saw you speak with anyone and felt sorry you were so alone. I never found out why you were there because by the time I came out of the change rooms, you were always gone. I wanted to speak to you in class, but didn't want to embarrass you with everyone else around. My, you have certainly changed."

Rick laughed. "Nature and a bit of hard work."

"What do you do now?"

"I'm currently a Senior Constable at Halmat Police Station, but I'm in my fourth year of law. I want my own law practice eventually. How about you?"

"I was studying Psychology but had to defer when I found out I was…" she didn't want to finish the sentence.

"You were pregnant with Dylan," he finished quietly.

"Yes. His father wanted the pregnancy terminated, but I refused and he left. I don't have the best luck with men. I recently broke up with a guy I'd been seeing for over a year because he said he wanted me, but not Dylan."

"Your parents said that's why you came out here."

"Yes, I needed to think, and it helps clear my head when I'm in the park. I'd given up on anyone finding me. It makes sense why you're here, but where are the rest of the police?"

"I'm alone. I was heading out for lunch yesterday when a poster tacked to a pole caught my attention. I recognised your face. My partner explained about your case back at the station, and since we had a couple of days off, I decided to speak to the two detectives in charge at the Narrabeen station. They agreed to me taking a look around since their search parties weren't having any luck. I hike in the park and know it well."

Rick stopped and took a mouthful of water before continuing. "Adam, one of the local Aborigines I called, agreed to help out today. He was adamant your presence could be felt around here and he was right. After we spotted you, he went back to alert the emergency services. I said I'd stay and take care of you overnight. They'll be back in the first thing in the morning."

"I can understand why no one would have thought to search on this side of the ravine since it wasn't where I'd told my parents I was going."

"No one had any idea you could be on this side. It explains why the dogs that were brought in couldn't pick up your scent."

"So why were you searching over on this side, there aren't any marked walking tracks? Why weren't you searching the track leading to the waterfall?"

"We were, but when we didn't find anything, Adam suggested we check along the edge of the ravine. He thought if you were caught in the slide, you might have grabbed onto what was left of one of the trees and take refuge on a ledge or in a cave. It was a long shot, but Adam was convinced you didn't get swept into the river. He said you wouldn't have survived and he could feel you. We kept calling your name, but you didn't answer. Obviously. Just on sunset, Adam caught sight of something red. We raced down the edge of the ravine until we were close enough to see it was you. I hiked back up the hill to the rope bridge, so I could cross over."

"I'm so glad you found me." Lyndsay was shaking with cold, probably shock had also set in, and her teeth were chattering.

"You're still freezing." Rick swept her onto his lap, leaned his back against the wall of the cave and pulled the blanket tighter around her as he cradled her close.

"Try and get some sleep."

Lyndsay snuggled into Rick's chest. Her shivering stopped and she drifted into sleep.

Chapter Four

Rick hadn't slept much with Lyndsay snug in his arms and her head resting over his pounding heart. All those years he'd dreamed of holding her in his arms and now those dreams had come true. He placed a kiss to the top of her head.

Throughout the night, Lyndsay had moaned in pain and a fever had developed. Although he'd given her some pills to control both, they hadn't been effective. He didn't like the look of her foot, it was swollen to bursting point, and the blue was beginning to turn black. It seemed to be getting worse by the hour. Getting medical help was becoming urgent.

The sun had barely poked its head over the horizon when Lyndsay opened her eyes and gazed at him with a sleepy expression.

"Hi," she murmured. Her head rested against Rick's chest.

He hoped that being able to hear his heartbeat throughout the night, and know she wasn't alone, had been comforting.

"Good morning. How are you feeling?"

"Better now you're with me," she smiled. "I have a lot of pain in my foot and I'm worried about it being numb. I feel hot, so I probably have an infection."

Rick made a decision, he sat her on the ground beside him and stood. "Would you like some water?"

"Yes, please but I need to relieve myself first," she said shyly.

Scooping her up, he sat her on the ledge outside the cave, hating the fact he needed to leave her alone while he gathered everything together.

Rick was stuffing things into his backpack when Lyndsay called out that she was ready to come back inside. Joining her outside, he offered her a bottle of water. She drank her fill and handed it back.

After taking a drink himself, he slipped the bottle into his backpack.

"I'm going to carry you back. With any luck, we'll meet up with the medics along the way. It will get you the help you need sooner."

He didn't give Lyndsay a chance to protest. After positioning his pack on his back, he swept her into his arms. She weighed no more than a feather and he wouldn't be slowed down.

***

Lyndsay wrapped her arms around Rick's neck and leaned into him as he trekked back up the mountain, before crossing the rope bridge to the other side where the main track was located. He moved at a brisk pace, his footing confident. She must have trusted his judgment Rick smiled when he noticed she'd drifted off.

"Rick, over here."

Rick glanced up. It was Adam with a couple of medics who were carrying a stretcher and medical bag. They were on the main track ahead.

"Hold up there. I'll come up to you." The track where they were was flatter and clear of any large debris.

"Okay," Adam called back.

"The cavalry's here," Rick smiled down at Lyndsay. "You'll be out of here in no time."

He covered the last few steps to the track and laid her gently on the waiting stretcher which had been placed flat on the ground.

Rick shook hands with Adam. "I thought I'd bring her up to save time."

"Good thinking," Adam introduced the medics. "This is John and Mark."

The two men glanced up from where they knelt while checking their patient. They nodded at Rick and he nodded back. "Thanks, guys."

"No problem," John said as he positioned Lyndsay's broken ankle into a plastic, blow-up cast. It would keep it immobilized for the trip to the hospital.

"Did you notify the police and her parents?" Rick asked Adam.

"Her parents are at the carpark and the Detectives asked if you could contact them later."

"Sure, thanks for that."

The medics gave Lyndsay a painkilling dispenser to use before strapping her firmly into the stretcher.

"We're ready to go," Mark said as both men stood.

"Let's get her out of here," Rick commanded.

Lyndsay held her hand out to Rick and he grasped it. "Thank you."

"You're welcome, honey."

They started back to the carpark where the ambulance would be waiting.

***

"Lyndsay." Joan rushed over as the stretcher was placed on the ground of the carpark while the medics unlocked the rear doors of the ambulance.

She dropped to her knees, and Rick watched as she hugged her daughter firmly. It gave him a great deal of satisfaction to know he'd returned Lyndsay back to her loving family. Tears poured from both women's eyes.

Alex approached his wife and daughter. Dylan held his Grandfather's hand but was pale and appeared scared.. As he neared his mother, he pulled his hand free and rushed toward Rick. Rick scooped him up.

"You found my Mummy. My Mummy's okay." Rick almost lost it when

Dylan placed his arms around his neck and smacked a kiss on his cheek. "Thank you, secret Santa."

Rick spoke around the lump in his throat, his voice hoarse. "Your Mummy is okay, but she has to go to the hospital because she has a sore foot. The doctors there will make it all better."

Dylan placed his tiny hands on each of Rick's cheeks and studied his face. "The hosipal will make it better?"

"Yes, they will buddy. How about you give Mummy a big hug and kiss before she goes? She really missed you."

Rick lowered the adorable little boy onto the ground and watched with a smile as his short legs scurried toward Lyndsay and he threw himself into her waiting arms.

Lyndsay peppered her sons face with kisses until he pushed her away.

"Mummy, Mr Police Officer is really secret Santa. He helps North Pole Santa. I was really good for ganma and ganpa and he brought you home for Christmas like he promised. He doesn't tell fibs like Ian."

Lyndsay gave Rick a look of gratitude that almost brought him to his knees. She mouthed her thanks before again hugging her son.

Mark and John had the ambulance ready and stood waiting. "We're ready. We need to get Miss Richards to the hospital now." John said.

"Where are you taking her?" Rick asked. His car was still in the carpark where he'd left it the previous day.

"We notified Mona Vale and they have a theatre ready. The Orthopedic Specialist should be there when we arrive." John informed everyone.

"We'll follow you down." Alex told Lyndsay.

Lyndsay turned toward Rick and extended her hand. "Will you come with me?"

"I'll take your car if you like." Adam offered. "I came with the medics, so I'll use it to get home. You can pick it up later. I'll text you my address."

"We can drop you off there when you're ready," Alex offered Rick.

Rick took the keys from his pocket, and after removing the car key, handed it to Adam. "Thanks, I'll call later and let you know what's happening." He waited while the medics lifted Lyndsay into the ambulance while her parents hovered nearby. Dylan now in his ganpa's arms.

"We'll see you there, darling," Joan called out to her daughter as Rick climbed into the back of the ambulance. The doors were closed firmly and the journey to the hospital began.

Lyndsay clutched Rick's hand as the ambulance sped through the streets with sirens blaring.

***

Rick paced the floor of the hospital waiting room while Lyndsay was in surgery. It had been almost six hours since she'd been taken into theatre.

Joan had taken a tired and irritable Dylan home, but Alex had remained.

"You're gonna wear a hole in the floor if you don't sit down soon, son."

Rick flopped into a chair. "She should have been out by now. Why has she been in there for so long?"

"You heard the doctor. It was a very bad break and he said it would be a long surgery."

Rick dragged his hand through his hair. He was tired, and desperately needed a shower, but he wasn't leaving until he knew Lyndsay was out of surgery and okay. "I know, but it doesn't make the waiting any easier."

Alex chuckled. "No, it doesn't. We're so grateful to you, Rick. I don't know how we would have coped if…if…" Tears filled his eyes.

Rick placed his hand on the older man's shoulder. "I'm glad I could help."

When a doctor in scrubs pushed through the double doors which led from the theatre suite, Rick and Alex jumped to their feet.

"Mr Richards?" The doctor asked as he stepped closer.

"Yes," Alex answered.

"Your daughter is doing well. We had to insert a plate and pins into the bones of her ankle. She'll have to wear a cast for about eight weeks and then she'll be required to have Physio. We expect she will be able to walk on it normally given time. She is very lucky that the foot didn't have to be amputated."

"She stayed off it, so didn't add to the damage," Rick informed.

The doctor nodded.

"It's probably what saved her foot."

"When can we see my daughter?"

"The nurses are getting her settled in recovery and then you can go in. I'll let them know you're waiting." The doctor removed his cap.

Alex shook the doctor's hand. "Thank you."

Before the surgeon left the room, Rick also thanked him and shook his hand.

Chapter Five

Lyndsay's eyes were closed when her father and Rick entered the recovery ward and crossed to the bed. Alex bent over and kissed his daughter's forehead. Her eyes fluttered open.

"Hi Dad," she said sleepily.

"Hi Sweetheart, how are you?"

"Tired and a bit sore. I need a shower."

Rick chuckled. "You and me both, babe."

Lyndsay held her hand out towards Rick and he gathered it gently into his. "You didn't have to stay, but I'm glad you did."

"I wanted to make sure you came through the surgery okay before I went home. I didn't know it was gonna take quite so long, though. I could have been home and back three times."

"I'm sorry," she said.

"Don't be. Your Dad and I kept each other company while we waited."

"Where's Mum and Dylan?" Lyndsay asked her father.

"The doctor said the surgery would take a while, so your mother took him home. I have to call her now and let her know she can come and see you."

"Ask her to bring Dylan, please?"

"Of course, honey. He'll want to see you as much as you want to see him." Alex kissed her again and shook Rick's hand. "Thanks again Rick. I hope we'll get to see more of you."

Rick watched Alex leave. *If I have any say in it you'll be seeing a lot more of me.* Having found his high school crush, he didn't intend letting her go anytime soon.

"Why don't you go too, Rick? There's nothing you can do here and you must be awfully tired. Won't your girlfriend/wife wonder where you are?"

"I have neither. Are you trying to get rid of me?"

"No, of course not but you don't really have any reason to stay."

"I have a very good reason to stay."

The expression on her face showed she was puzzled.

"I like you, Lyndsay. I've had a giant crush on you for years but was too scared to say anything. When we finished with school, and went our separate ways, I was heartbroken for a long time. I'd very much like to date you. We can go out for dinner, to the movies, dancing. I want to be with you, get to know you better now I've found you again."

A shadow passed over her beautiful face. "What about my son?"

"Apart from the dancing, he's included. I'd love for the three of us to go out together, we could go to fun parks and arcades that little boys love. But, now and again, it would be nice to spend time alone."

"Are you sure?"

"Absolutely. Your parents said Dylan's father didn't want anything to do with him, I'd like to show him not all men are selfish ratbags."

Lyndsay squeezed his hand and smiled. Her whole face lit up and her eyes sparkled. "I'd love that but we might have to put the dancing on hold for a while." She pointed to her ankle which was encased in white plaster.

"I can wait." *I've waited this long.*

"Where have you been? Why wasn't I dating you instead of all the other jerks?"

"You wouldn't have that sweet little boy if it wasn't for one jerk." Despite himself, Rick yawned.

"It's late darlin', go home, have a shower and get some sleep," Lyndsay almost ordered.

"I'll come back tomorrow morning, but if you need me before then, call." He scribbled his mobile number on the back of one of his police business cards and handed it to her.

"Thank you."

Rick leaned forward to give her a kiss on the cheek. Lyndsay placed a hand on the back of his head and pulled him toward her. She captured his lips in a soul searing kiss. Their tongues twisted and danced as he held her close. When they separated, their eyes locked.

"Wow!"

"Wow is right," he smiled. "I'll see you in the morning."

Lyndsay watched as he left, her fingers lightly brushing over her lips.

***

Rick's mobile rang as he locked the door to his unit. "Masters," he answered while jiggling the key out of the lock.

"Rick, it's Alex Richards."

"Alex, what can I do for you?"

"Lyndsay asked me to give you a call and let you know the doctor is allowing her to come home."

"I was just leaving to go there. I thought they were going to keep her for a couple of days." Rick was disappointed he wouldn't be seeing more of her in the hospital where he was free to come and go as he pleased.

"Lyndsay refused to stay, she misses Dylan. The doctor agreed as long as she stays with her mother and I until she's able to get around by herself. That seemed to satisfy him. I thought you'd be going there this morning, would it be any trouble for you to pick her up?"

"None at all, I'd love to bring her home."

"You'll need to swing past her house and pick up a few things for her, Lyndsay will tell you what she needs. We have everything here for Dylan."

"That won't be a problem. Happy to be of help."

"We'll see you both here a bit later then, and Rick?"

"Yes?"

"You're welcome in our home any time Lyndsay wants you here."

"Thank you."

Rick disconnected the call and descended the staircase with a spring in his step. Happier now he realised he was welcome in Lyndsay's family home.

***

Lyndsay was dressed in a pretty blue dress which matched her eyes and was seated in a wheelchair beside the bed when Rick arrived. He leaned over and kissed her cheek gently.

"Good morning. I hear you needed a cop to break you out of the joint?"

Lyndsay laughed. "I thought cops were supposed to make sure you stayed in the joint?"

Rick shrugged. "Let's just say this is one lady who deserves to be busted free."

Lyndsay laughed again, a sound he'd never tire of hearing. "Obviously you're here to take me home."

"Yep. Your Dad rang to tell me you were being turned loose and asked if I would mind coming to get you. I was on my way here, so of course I said I would."

"Thank you."

"Rick Masters at your service, ma'am." He stumbled over a dropped pill container as he bowed low, causing Lyndsay to laugh. He regained his balance and smiled at her. "Good to see you find humor in my clumsiness."

"I'm sorry," she laughed. "But you looked hilarious."

"Hmmm, doesn't sound like you're too sorry. Shall we fly this coop?"

"Yes, please. Could you get the nurse and tell her. I've signed all the papers and my meds are in the bag." She pointed to a small bag on the bed.

"Be right back." He disappeared in the direction of the nurses station.

Lyndsay sighed. Despite her broken ankle, and various other aches and pains, she was the happiest she had been in a very long time. Was it because of Rick? Was she attracted to him?

You bet I'm attracted to him, how could any woman not be? He was kind, funny, and gentle.

Why the hell wasn't he engaged, married, or have a partner?

Lyndsay was still questioning herself when Rick sauntered back into the room.

"Okay sweetheart, we're out of here." He placed the crutches provided by the hospital across her lap and the bag over the handle of the chair. After releasing the brake, he pushed her toward the lift where a nurse joined them to escort Lyndsay out..

The lift descended rapidly, stopping on the ground floor with a jolt and Rick wheeled Lyndsay over to the entry door in the foyer. He applied the brake. "Wait here and I'll bring the car up."

She laughed. "I'll be here. I can't exactly run away."

Rick darted through the doors to recover his car from the carpark.

There was a long circular drive up to the entry where patients could be dropped off and collected. He stopped the car and sprinted inside. Lyndsay was talking to the nurse while she waited.

"Ready?"

"Very," she answered, and attempted to push herself up.

"I'll take it from here, nurse. Thank you." Rick swooped in, placed an arm under her knees and another around her back. The crutches clattered to the floor as he lifted her against his broad chest.

"Oops," he looked sheepishly at the nurse who stood nearby. "I'll come back for those and the bag."

"I'll bring them out," the nurse offered as she stooped and picked them up before taking the bag from the back of the chair. She followed him through the main glass doors and stood patiently while he lowered Lyndsay into the passenger seat of his car.

Rick recovered the items from the nurse, thanked her, and placed them into the back seat. He then climbed behind the wheel and drove away.

"Nice car," Lyndsay glanced around at her surroundings.

"I like it. Always wanted one, so saved the money I earned working at Maccas while I was at school, added money I saved working as a cop, and bought it about three months ago. Better than the old beat up Holden I was driving around."

"Better than my old Ford Fiesta that's for sure."

"I saw it in the carpark on the day I came to search for you. It looked like it belongs on the scrapheap." Rick drove down the traffic laden Pittwater Road toward Lyndsay's house.

"When you have a child, you have other priorities, but I guess I'll have to bite the bullet and get something a bit safer."

"As a cop, I would recommend it. I don't know how you passed rego. As a person who likes you, and your son, I would plead with you to get something safer."

She laughed. "You sound like Mum and Dad. Where are we going?"

"Your Dad asked me to take you to your place first so you could pick up a few things."

"How do you know where I live?"

"You told me during the night we were in the cave."

"Oh, I was a bit out it at the time, but I do remember you saying you have a unit in Collaroy that overlooks the beach. I would love to see it one day."

You will, babe. If it's up to me, you will.

"I would love to have you and Dylan over for a barbecue lunch or dinner. I have a barbie out on the balcony which faces over the beach. I could sit there for hours and watch the waves crash onto the shore."

"Sounds perfect," she sighed.

"Here we are." Rick pulled the car into the driveway of her brick weatherboard house with a beautiful cottage garden. He jumped out, rushed around the back of the car, and opened Lyndsay's door.

"I need my bag. The keys to the house are in there." Lyndsay pointed to where it sat on the back seat.

Rick plucked it from the seat and waited while she rummaged in the overfilled bag for her keys. She held them up in the air, triumphant.

"Found them."

He carefully lifted her into his arms and strode to the front door. Lyndsay inserted the key and threw the door open.

"Where to?" he asked.

"Down that hall, first door on the left." She pointed ahead of where they stood.

Rick followed her directions and deposited her onto a large four posted bed. He glanced around the room which most definitely belonged to a female.

The bed was dressed in a soft lilac quilt with matching pillows. A white woven blanket was draped over the base. The linen window curtains were white trimmed with lilac. The room was light and sunny. A large lilac rug lay on the floor by the bed. It was a tastefully decorated, very feminine room.

Lyndsay blushed. She was embarrassed to have this gorgeous hunk witnessing her most private of rooms. She had brought no-one in here, slept with no-one since Dylan's father. He'd been a one-night stand after drinking too much at a party held at her girlfriend's home.

It was probably why her last relationships had soured, she'd refused to allow Ian to stay in her home. She had promised herself, the next time she took a man into her bed, he would be her husband.

"How many other men have been in this room?"

Lyndsay's head snapped up at the abrupt question. She was angered and hurt but was Rick jealous?. And if so, why?

"You're the first since Dylan's father…except for Dad. Do you think I'm some kind of loose woman?"

Rick blushed with embarrassment. "Sorry, didn't mean to say that out loud. It wasn't meant the way it sounded. I know you're not that kind of girl, but it drives me crazy that another man might have been in here. I mean..."

He is jealous! "Rick, stop now before you dig yourself a hole too deep to climb out of."

His face reddened and he kept his mouth shut before saying anything that would embarrass him further.

Lyndsay changed the subject, letting Rick off the hook. "There's a suitcase in the bottom of the wardrobe. Could you pull it out and place it on the bed for me?" Rick jumped at the opportunity to diffuse the situation and pulled a large black case from the wardrobe. He set it on the bed, pulled the zippers around and lay it open.

"Would you open both lots of doors, so I can make a decision about what I want?"

He opened the four wardrobe doors and stood back. Man, the woman had some clothes. She could open her own shop.

Lyndsay began pointing out what she would like. Dresses—casual and dressy, pants, tops, cardigans, and jumpers. Rick carefully folded them into the case.

"That's all from there. In the bottom drawer of the chest, I'd like all my shorts."

Rick pulled out what appeared to be dozens of pairs of shorts, some of them looked awfully skimpy, but he found himself wanting to see her wear them. He removed clothing from drawers as requested under Lyndsay's watchful eyes. Only the top two smaller drawers were left.

Lyndsay blushed. "Just tip the top two drawers into the suitcase." She twisted her fingers in her lap.

Rick pulled open the first drawer. Bras—sexy, lacy, see-through, greeted his eyes and he reddened. He quickly guessed what was in the other drawer. He tipped the contents of both into the case and gazed at Lyndsay for his next set of instructions.

Perfume, brush, comb, hair bibs and bobs were all added.

Lyndsay took one last look around and was satisfied she hadn't forgotten anything.

"That's all. You can close it now."

Rick closed the bulging suitcase, set it on its wheels on the floor ,and pulled up the handle. "I'll put this in the car and come back for you.

Lyndsay smiled as he left.

Minutes later Rick was back. Lifting her back into his arms, he started for the car. Halfway down the hall, Lyndsay spoke.

"Rick, stop."

He stopped and peered down at her.

She pulled his head down to hers and captured his lips. He groaned as nerve endings throughout his body exploded and his dick hardened. His tongue danced with hers and he realized, Lyndsay had the ability to bring him to his knees with one simple kiss.

One way or another, Lyndsay would be his. He would treat her the way she deserved to be treated. She was his princess.

Chapter Six

Rick carried Lyndsay up the front steps of her parents' home, and on reaching the front door, she leaned forward and threw it open.

"Mum, Dad, Dylan. We're here," she shouted excitedly.

Rick heard Dylan's feet clattering on the wood flooring as he ran. "Mummy, Mummy. I missed you." The little boy jumped up and down in front of them, his arms reaching out.

"Bring her through to the living room please, Rick," Joan instructed.

Rick deposited her on the lounge with her broken ankle resting on pillows that had been set in place to elevate the leg and positioned cushions behind her. "I'll go and get you suitcase and crutches from the car."

"Thank you." Lyndsay smiled.

Dylan bounced up onto his mother and threw his arms around her neck. He placed kisses all over her face which caused her to laugh. "You did miss me, didn't you?" She sat her little boy on her stomach.

"I missed you this much," he stretched his arms wide.

"I missed you too, darling." Tears sprang to her eyes, she'd been terrified that she would never see him again. Thank God Rick had found her.

The man of the hour sauntered back into the living room. "Your Dad has taken your suitcase to your room."

Rick lifted Lyndsay's legs, sat on the couch, and lowered them across his lap. A shiver washed over her when he placed his hands lightly on her thighs, and Rick glanced at her with concern.

"Are you cold?"

"No, I'm fine." She glanced down at his hands.

Rick followed her eyes and gave her a knowing smile. When her parents entered the room, and noticed how their daughter and Rick were sitting, eyebrows were raised in unison.

"Coffee?" Joan asked.

Rick accepted since he was in no hurry to leave. "That would be very nice, thank you."

Alex sat opposite and eyed the new man in his daughter's life.

"Lyndsay explained that you were the boy she used to tell us about who watched her practice and play netball at school. She said you always sat alone in the stands, and it made her feel sad. She didn't know you were there for her. Apparently you were short, chubby, and wore glasses back then."

"Yep, that was me. It was Lyndsay I was there for, but I was too scared to say anything. She was so beautiful and I was the school nerd. The school joke."

Joan settled a tray of coffee mugs on the small table. "That's so sad, Rick. No one has the right to make someone else feel that way. I'm sorry that happened to you."

"I should have tried harder to be your friend."

I shrugged at Lyndsay's comment. "I survived and it wasn't that bad."

"Milk, sugar?" Janet held the milk jug in her hand towards Rick.

'Just white, thank you." Rick answered.

Joan poured in the milk and handed him the mug before handing one to Lyndsay and sitting next to her husband. Dylan scrambled onto her lap.

"You're certainly not, short and chubby now." She bestowed a benevolent smile on him.

"No, ma'am. I grew up pretty good and I wear contacts."

"How long have you been in the Police Force," Alex asked.

"Going on four years now. I'm in my fourth year of law, and hopefully, I'll have my own law practice one day."

"You've done well for yourself."

"Yes, I've worked hard to succeed."

"How long do you have off, Rick?" Lyndsay asked.

"I go back to work on the afternoon shift tomorrow."

"So your days off have been taken up searching, and caring, for our daughter," Joan said.

"I don't mind. I didn't have plans. Alex, with your permission, I would like to date Lyndsay and Dylan."

Alex sputtered and the sip of coffee he'd just taken ended up down the front of his shirt. Joan dabbed at the mess with a napkin.

"Alex, please be careful," she admonished.

"Sorry darling, I've never been asked permission by someone to date my daughter *and* grandson. No one has even asked my permission to date my daughter!"

Rick turned his head and smiled at Lyndsay. "The way I see it, they're a package deal. A very nice one at that."

Dylan's eyes ping-ponged back and forth between the adults. He was trying hard to understand because he knew what they were saying must have something to do with him. They kept mentioning his name.

"What's date mean?" he asked.

"It means Rick wants to take you and your mummy out sometimes," Alex explained.

Dylan whipped his head around to face his mother. "Can we Mummy? I like Rick. Can we pleeeease go date him?"

The adults laughed at his innocence.

"I guess if it's okay with Grandpa." Lyndsay teased.

"Pleeeease, Ganpa?" Dylan pleaded.

"Of course you can." Alex agreed.

"Yippee, we can date you, Rick." He clapped his hands before throwing his arms in the air.

"Sit still darling, you'll spill grandma's coffee," Joan said.

Dylan quieted.

"Thank you, I promise I'll take good care of them both."

"Yes, I think you will. Thank you for asking for my permission. It's very old-fashioned thinking for a young man to ask a father if he can date his daughter."

"It's respect, Alex, and I was raised to show respect and courtesy." Rick grasped

Lyndsay's hand and focused on her face. "I'm sorry you had an accident and were injured but I'm glad I happened upon your missing poster and was the one to find you. I've been given a second chance to make you mine and this time I'm not letting you get away." He lifted her hand to his lips and gently kissed her fingers.

Lyndsay blushed. "I hope not."

Alex squeezed his wife's hand. "I have no doubt, Rick, you are the man for our daughter.

"I hope so. I really hope so."

***

Christmas Day

Rick headed towards the front door of Lyndsay's parent's home, his arms filled with gifts. Dylan watched through the window and when he disappeared from sight, Rick grinned.

The past few days had been better than he could have ever imagined and he knew without any doubt, Lyndsay was the woman meant to be his wife.

Dylan threw open the front door and jumped up and down with excitement.

"Rick, come and see the train set Santa brung me. I got books, pencils, games." He jammed his tiny hands on his hips and sighed. "There's just so much for you to see. Hurry up."

"I need you to move out of the doorway, bud."

"Oh, yeah."

The excited child stepped back and Rick strode through to where the living room had once been, it currently resembled a toy shop.

"Is one of those for me, Rick?"

"It certainly is."

Rick set the parcels on the floor, sat on the carpet, and handed Dylan the largest. He dropped his backside to the carpet and ripped at the wrapping paper in excitement. When the box was revealed, he squealed with delight and held it up for his mother to see.

"Mummy, look! I can be a policeman like Rick now. It has handcuffs and a gun. Can I put it on?"

"Of course you can darling."

Dylan pulled Rick by the hand, wanting his help. Rick snagged him around the waist and held him in place.

"Hold up, I want to speak with mummy and then I'll help."

"Okay."

Setting him off to one side, Rick crawled to where Lyndsay sat, and gathered her hand. You could have heard a pin drop in the silence.

"Lyndsay, I knew you were the woman for me from the first time I laid eyes on you as a twelve-year-old boy starting high school. It's taken me a while, but I have finally found the courage to say what is in my heart. I love you, honey. There will never be anyone else for me. I'd be honored if you would consent to being my wife and allowing me to become Dylan's father. To be by your side as we guide him and our other children through life."

Rick removed a red velvet box from his pocket and snapped the lid open to reveal Lyndsay's favorite stone. A solitaire diamond cut blood ruby set in platinum on a platinum band.

Tears filled her eyes and Rick heard sniffles behind him. He'd asked her father the previous night for his permission to marry his daughter and Alex had readily agreed.

"Mummy, say yes, I want Secret Santa Rick to be my Daddy."

Lyndsay burst into tears as she shouted, YES, and after slipping the ring onto her finger, Rick gathered her into my arms.

"I love you so much Secret Santa. This has been the best Christmas of my life."

"Mine too."

As we kissed, Dylan shouted and yelled about how he finally had a Daddy who was *cool*.

Life was pretty much perfect and Rick owed it all to a chance sighting of a fifty cent poster.

THE END

About the Author

I'm an Australian author who writes in a variety of genres, including Western romance, historical romance, Gay Romance, and contemporary romance.

I have published over 60 books and novellas, many of which feature strong, independent heroines and rugged, alpha male heroes. Some of my popular series include the Outback Australia series and The Carter Brothers series.

My books are known for their well-researched historical details and vivid descriptions of the Australian landscape.

My work has garnered praise from readers and critics alike, and I have won several awards for my writing.

If you're interested in learning more about my books:

Linktree

https://linktr.ee/SusanHorsnell

For Australian Historical Romance written under Annabel Vaughan

https://linktr.ee/annabelvaughan

Milton Keynes UK
Ingram Content Group UK Ltd.
UKHW020250221123
432980UK00016B/853